# Lost in Space

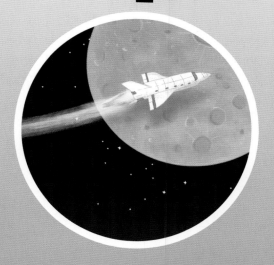

written by **Anne Giulieri**

illustrated by Gary Cherrington

Kane was happy to be at the museum
with Dad and Nana.
But Layla was not.

"Look," said Kane.
"I can see some dinosaur bones."

"I don't like dinosaurs," said Layla.

"There are many other things
at the museum," said Dad.
"Maybe you will see something you like."

As Dad went to get a map,
Nana and the children looked around.

3

People began to line up near
a big black door.

"It's getting busy," said Layla.

"There must be something good
behind that door," said Kane.

The door opened, and everyone began
to go inside.

"Let's take a quick look, too," said Nana.

Kane, Layla and Nana found themselves in a big room.

"There's nothing in here," said Layla.

All of a sudden, the lights went off.

# Clunk!

The door shut, and everyone was quiet.

"Oh, no," cried Layla with her eyes shut tight.
"It's very dark in here,
and now we have lost Dad!"

"Hold my hand," said Nana.
"You don't need to be scared."

Layla laid her head on Nana
with her eyes still shut tight.

"You should open your eyes, Layla,"
said Kane.

Layla slowly looked up from Nana.

"Look at all the stars!" said Layla.

the Moon, too!" said Nana.

...den, a spaceship zoomed past.

"This is fun!" said Kane.
"I wish we could stay here all day."

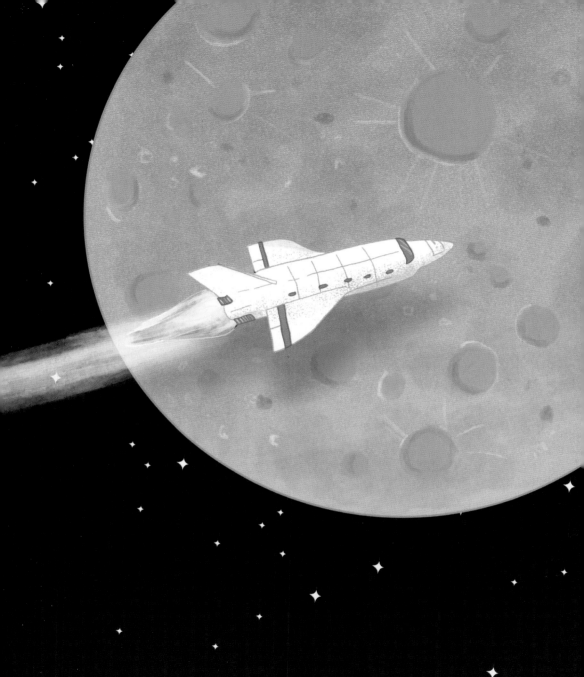

"Look!" said Kane. "There's planet Earth. It's blue and green."

"Yes," said Layla, "And I can see seven other planets, too!"

"Can you see the Sun?" asked Nana.

"It looks like a big ball of fire," said Kane.

"This is great!" said Layla. "It's not scary."

Just then, there was a big
# BANG!

Everyone looked at the door.
A dark shape began to walk over
to Kane and Layla.

"**AAHH!!**" they both shouted.

15

"Don't be scared," laughed Dad.
"It's just me!"

"You found us!" said Kane.

"We were lost in space," laughed Layla.
"But it was lots of fun!"